TiANNA

Thank you for you...

MAny wishes, MAny blessings

to you Now & in the future...

Love Always!!

LOSER

LOSER

LUIS MARTINEZ
Xulon Press

Xulon Press
2301 Lucien Way #415
Maitland, FL 32751
407.339.4217
www.xulonpress.com

Edited by Xulon Press.

Printed in the United States of America.

ISBN-13: 9781545619612

Table of Contents

No Trespassing

*I*f you're asking yourself why I chose this title, the answer is very simple. It's the air between you and me. I'm not the type to allow just anyone to get that close to me, or to even get to know the real me. Shit, sometimes I feel like I don't even know the real me. Today, I may do things one way, and tomorrow, I will do the complete opposite. I live with my guard up every second of the day. I've been like that since I was a teenager. It's stressful that I live that way because I confuse even myself with some of the choices I make, but it's what works for me. But like an addict, most of my choices only lead me to regret as I continue to relapse again and again. Even after all that, somehow I manage to do everything drug-free. I've never been the type to use drugs or turn to alcohol like many around me have when they couldn't handle their problems. Well, I wasn't necessarily entirely drug free, but it wasn't a real problem. My problem is that I just continue making the same mistakes over and over again and expect the outcome to be different. When I say that I relapse, what I mean is that every time I gave something a shot or someone the opportunity to get to know the real me, somehow, someway, I ended up regretting it.

It became so hard for me to open up to people that at one point many really thought there was something wrong with me. From one day to the next, I just shut down. I went from having fun every day and enjoying life to a person no one wanted to be next to. Not too many people will admit this, but I will. This was all due to being young and ignorant. I thought I knew better, so, regardless of what people told me, I did whatever I wanted to do, no matter what, just to piss people off. When I turned around one day and didn't see anyone there pushing me to do right I felt alone. But I couldn't show it because it would have been a weakness people would have laughed at me for. I was acting like I was a grown man who could handle the business of grown men. All because I couldn't handle the pressure that people were constantly putting on me.

It got to the point where everything that I thought was a positive was being shot down. So, instead of being positive all the time, I felt I would get more attention by trying to do the opposite. It's funny how that works. It wasn't until I began to argue back and express how I felt about things that I started to get the attention I always wanted. Unfortunately, the attention I was getting came with many consequences. Just for the hell of it, I would disagree with someone else's point of view—even when they were right. When you're young and stupid, you feel like there is no one in this world who can tell you anything different once you have already made up your mind. But I didn't just have a problem with my upbringing. Once I became rebellious, I had a problem with everything. I had a problem with religion, school, sports, the streets, and even things that were none of my business to even care about. I even had a problem with the way things were going on around the world. So, not only was I saying fuck the police, I was also saying fuck the president, too. The real crazy thing about it, though, is that I really learned a lot from being rebellious. I learned the harder way, but I learned.

It's really hard for me to admit that I was wrong a lot. It takes a real man to admit when they are wrong. But my reasons for doing the wrong things had nothing to do with thinking they were right or because it somehow benefited me. I was just being rebellious. I began to hate having so many people on my back trying to tell me how to be. One mistake that a lot of adults do make is assuming that a younger person, who hasn't gone through what they have gone through, expects them to know what they know. I hear parents calling their own kids stupid for not knowing right from wrong when they themselves were the role models who led them to making those wrong decisions. The same thing goes for all those teachers that were constantly telling us that we would always be losers living in the projects because of the way we were acting.

When you sit back and allow people to control you and tell you what they think is right or wrong for you, you sort of feel like you're just living your life the way others want you to live it. Once you start doing things your way, you feel a little more powerful. But once that power makes you feel untouchable, that's when life begins testing your strength. And believe me, I was tested a lot. But even when I failed, I still learned my lessons. Arguing and debating became part of my everyday life. I would challenge everything and everyone that tried to tell me anything. Most took it as me just being an asshole or someone who just thought knew it all, but in reality, I was just trying to find the right answers to make sense of all my own questions. To this day, people avoid getting into a conversation with me because of the way I challenge their opinions. Honestly, it's really just one less headache I have to deal with. It keeps me from having to deal with their issues, too.

One thing that I am really bad at is keeping promises. I hate having to answer to anybody. I know that people are continuously telling me what they think is right for me and that I should take advantage of it, but it's just not in me to accept anything unless I feel comfortable with it. That's why I try my hardest not to ever make any promises or put myself in situations where people are going to feel that I'm just lying to them. I have been so used to doing everything for myself and on my own terms that I never really pay any attention to what others expect from me. I do admit this: I can be a real miserable fuck sometimes. No one has to remind me of that. I can go days without answering my phone or leaving my house—just to avoid having to deal with anything or anyone. Many tell me that I have split personalities and that I suffer from depression. I wouldn't call it depression. Call it what you want to call it. To me, I really just don't want to be bothered when I'm in one of my moods.

Let me explain how I got to this point in my life. Honestly, I only figured it out while I was writing this book. I have tried to figure out why I always reacted so violently or negatively when others tried to get in my way. Some of the things that I will mention may offend some people I know, but at least I'm opening up a bit to allow them to know some things they might have questioned. I have confused many people who thought they knew me best. I have allowed many who were close to me to distance themselves because of the way I treated them or reacted to them when all they ever tried to do was help me. Although writing this may not help me change my personal way of being, it will at least help me feel more comfortable mentally, knowing and accepting that I have been wrong many times. It took me many years to understand that it takes two or more people to agree in order for anything that I say or think to become a fact. You try to figure it out.

Paranoia

*H*ave I ever made mistakes? Of course I have. More than you would think. I've made choices I knew had many consequences I probably wouldn't be able to deal with. I think most of us have at one point or another. I hated authority more than anything. I guess I started being that way because my dad was always on top of everything I did. I hated authority so much I even began to hate being told what to do by my teachers in school. I talk about my dad and not too many people really understand what it was like for me growing up. I look back now and I understand what his intentions were. But if you think that I was going to walk out of my house to be told what to do and how to be by every other adult I came across, you were wrong. That's when I began being rebellious. I got to the point where I didn't care if you were a teacher, a coach, or even a cop. I lost my respect for all authority because my dad was so hard on me for reasons I couldn't understand at the time. And because he was my dad, he was the only one I felt I had to respect. What made it even worse was that I never really ever knew what I was being punished for because my parents never really took the time to explain anything to me. It was always "because I said so" or "because you don't pay any bills here."

I'm not trying to blame my issues on my parents—far from it. I'm just trying to explain why I became so anti-authority at such an early age. Everywhere I went I felt paranoid. It felt like every time I made a decision to do what I thought was right I was being told I was doing it wrong. So one day, I just said fuck it. I'm just gonna do whatever I felt was right and not even care about the consequences. It was my way of making me happy. Once I started doing whatever I wanted to do all of a sudden people began to worry. Everywhere I went people were asking me, "What's wrong?" or, "Are you OK?" And the only one question that I kept asking myself was where were you when I tried to do the right things?

By the time I got around to junior high, there was not one adult that could tell me anything. I was an A and B student all the way up through my elementary school years.

When I got around other teens that didn't have parents like I did, I began feeling like my parents were the worst. Students were getting suspended, skipping school, getting F's on their report cards and here I am, worried about being yelled at for the little things. My dad was so hard on me that I honestly think I lost the love for the only thing I ever really did care about: I was a diehard baseball player. It was the only thing I felt I could do right. But even when I got up to the plate I couldn't really concentrate. My dad would stand right behind the fence and yell at me if I didn't stand correctly or hit the ball the right way. It got to the point where I began striking out on purpose just so I would be left alone. When the coaches would yell at me for bunting even when they never gave the sign, I stopped listening to them, too. I took my uniform off and quit right in the dugout. So love has really never worked for me. I loved my parents growing up, but hated them by the time I became a teenager. I loved school, but stopped caring because B's weren't good enough for my dad. I loved sports, but quit because I was tired of being told what to do and how to do it. Shit, I even loved life until everyone got on my case about every little thing I did.

I guess I couldn't reach all their high expectations—no matter how hard I tried.

Looking back, I wish I wasn't such a punk and would have just accepted every battle I went through as motivation. I used to think that people were on my back because they hated me. Now I realize that it was the complete opposite. I am where I am today because I never really understood why I was being pushed to do everything right. Instead, I felt I was being punished for not doing things other people's way. I felt like I was too good to be coached or to be told what to do. I began listening to all those junior high dropouts and drug dealing inmates and wanted to be just like them. In their world, the only people that could tell them what to do were cops and judges. But they had to be caught first. I loved the rush of being chased. It felt better than being caught between the bases on a baseball field. Deep inside I knew that it really wasn't the right thing to do but the streets was the only place where no one could criticized me for doing things my way.

Ever since I began to do things my way I've been lost. I began to live a double life. It's been a mixture of regrets and having to deal with my day-to-day struggles. But since I brought myself to this point, I have no one to point the finger at but myself. I just deal with my fuck ups and have sort of accepted it as a challenge to somehow making things right on the day-to-day basis. I try every day to never look back. It's just hard when I really know that I could have been doing much better today had I just listened. I confused discipline with authority and became rebellious, simple as that. I messed up and I take all responsibility for it. Unfortunately, I now feel like a stranger in my own life. I think a certain way, but tend to still act rebelliously. I became so addicted to doing things the wrong way that I sometimes fear doing it the right way. By that, I mean being taken advantage of. It's the only thing I hate about my decision-making. I feel like everyone is still out to get me, or that they will confuse my kindness for weakness. That's why I'm an asshole to most until they get to really know the real me.

Loner

I have come to the conclusion that I truly do live a confusing life. Most of the things I preach, I tend to do the opposite. Most of the things I do, I end up regretting. In fact, most of the times I really do wish I could just stay sleeping and dreaming instead of living and stressing. I live a paranoid life. I'm constantly thinking something is going to happen to me. I waste so much time keeping my guard up that I don't even pay attention to what's right in front of me. You would think that I have amnesia or Alzheimer's disease because I can't really remember anything other than what's happening in my life now. What happened to me yesterday is irrelevant. I could have had the best time of my life today with people and the next day act as if it never occurred because I went right back to my alone time. This happens to me especially in relationships. People always tell me I'm afraid of love and commitment, but that's not it. I just don't build with anyone like I used to. There is something inside of me not allowing me to get that close to anyone.

I do think I spend too much of my life chasing after every regret I have dealt with to try to change it all rather than learning from the experience. I know there is nothing I can do to change the past, but in my head I try to relive those moments and see what I could have done differently. In all honesty, I have felt like I've lived a lie for most of my life. What's sad is that I only lied to avoid hurting people. It was never to benefit. Unfortunately, each and every time I did try to tell people the truth they wanted answers I could never really explain. I usually went with how I felt but they could never understand why from one minute to the next I felt the opposite way. I have lived the complete opposite of how I truly feel and think. I have always known and pictured what I have always wanted, but I have never fully been satisfied to the point where I've been comfortable with being happy. I have lived this fantasy life in my head that has turned into a major disaster. I guess it's true when they say that we should just live life instead of going out searching for things that really aren't meant for us to have.

In case you ever wondered why I was always so moody all the time, it was my only way of showing you that I wanted to be left alone. It was never personal. I go through things that I know no one is able to help me through so I just shut down until it all goes away. Unfortunately, it would always come back. People always took it as if I didn't like them or I had something against them when I shut down. All I ever wanted was to be left alone until I was able to think straight again without being distracted. Instead, people kept pushing me for answers I couldn't give them. It was a mood that just took over my entire body. I must admit, the death of my ex-girlfriend really took a toll in my life. It was tough for me to not only deal with it but also to accept it and move on. I still have not fully grieved. There is something inside of me that is not allowing me to. I remember dialing her phone number the next day and getting her voicemail with her saying that she was unable to get to the phone at this time. The sad part about it was that she would never be able to ever again. I just wanted to hear her voice one last time. Her voice is stuck in my head till this day.

Sometimes, I wish I could start all over again. I keep going back to the day when she passed away. If I've ever regretted anything in my life, it was how I went about dealing with her before her death. If you don't believed that you never know what you had until you lose it, try losing someone you really cared about without having closure. You'll definitely find out how important the person you lose really was when they are gone. It's usually not until you cross the line of regret that you realize you've gone too far. And that's what life becomes for people who lose loved ones on bad terms. That's a tough lesson you will really never learn from. Unfortunately, you can never go back and change any of it.

The weirdest dream I ever woke up from was when I was doing her funeral ceremony by myself all over again. I was the only one at the funeral home. Somehow, I ended up bringing her casket to the cemetery and doing the burial myself. There are many times when I see her in my dreams and I keep asking her for her phone number but she keeps turning me down. Many people would probably wake up confused, but I cherish the dreams. Her death has been and probably will be the worst thing I will ever go through. I'm constantly being reminded of it all because I have to drive by the scene of the accident on my way to work. Each time, I say a prayer in my head for her in hopes that she's okay where she is. She has been in my thoughts almost every second of my life after the accident. Even when she wasn't, something would always remind me to think of her. It got to the point where I could not sleep no matter how tired I was. I began to abuse painkillers by the dozens. No one ever knew because even when I was around certain people at night, I wouldn't tell them. I would just fall asleep as normal.

Here are a few hints about when I was feeling worthless. If you ever saw me riding around town numerous times, it was usually when I couldn't just stay at home because I was going crazy being stressed out. If you ever saw me just sitting around not talking and you asked me why I was so quiet and I told you that nothing was wrong, chances are I was lying. If you ever saw me driving by you and I was wearing sunglasses, which I never really wear, it was usually when I came from the cemetery or I was listening to a song that reminded me of someone who is no longer here. I had to hide my tears. I never wanted anyone to know when things were bothering me. But if you ever saw me walking around with my hands in my pockets, it would always be when I saw someone I didn't trust or know and I was holding on to a gun just in case.

I hated the feeling of always having to do that, which is the real reason why I no longer hang out in places where I would have to feel that way.

Since her death, I have felt dead inside. Like my heart was buried with her underground. I've been stuck between dreams and wishes ever since. I have a difficult time trying to find a way to escape my past. The only thing that makes me feel alive is the knowledge that I am walking and breathing. I'm an example of an individual that you would look at and say that I seem to be living the perfect life. But we all know that everyone has personal issues in their lives. If you don't, you are not living. Some issues are worse than others, but everyone deals with them differently. My problem is a little more difficult to resolve because I hold on to guilt instead of accepting it and moving on.

I consider myself a good person. I'm the type of person who would do anything for anyone at any given time. I wasn't always like that, but throughout my life I have seen so many people going through some of the same types of struggles I have faced and feel like I can help heal their problems. I regret a lot of the choices I have made that have hurt others, but none of them were intentional. My anxiety comes from having to do what is right for me, and having to do it the right way. Before, I did things the wrong way, which made things happen a lot faster with quicker results. So it does bother me to be patient.

There are only a handful of people who ever really understood me. They knew some of my deepest thoughts and feelings. But I would never want anyone to ever have to feel sorry for me while I'm here or when I'm gone. I have caused all of the drama in my own life. There are many others who have struggled without a choice that may need that attention. This is something I really hate to admit, but I strongly feel that there is nothing anyone in this world could ever do for me to make me happy. I've gotten pretty much everything I have ever wanted in my life, but most of it has only satisfied me momentarily. My problem has always been that while I try my hardest to adapt to the people I accept in my life, something always happens to keep me from committing to them. Unfortunately, it comes out of nowhere and they have to end up hurting because my decision came so unexpectedly.

What makes us who we are is how people perceive us. If they stand by you, it may mean that they like and appreciate you for who you are. If they don't, it usually means you've done something to offend them or they simply just can't find a way to get along with you. But one major reason why people have issues is simply because they don't understand each other. Friendship is no different than having a relationship with someone; it is mostly about communication. If you can deal with a person for who they are or what they do and you decide to stick around and deal with it then you have accepted them for who they are. Unfortunately, everyone I've come across wants me to change my ways to satisfy them. Here's the other side to how I really think.

People plan at an early age for what they want to become in life. Some choose to become athletes while others choose a career they think will pay off. The rest rely on religion or trying to get lucky somehow. I was one of them. I've been through all the above at one point in my life. None of them worked, so I chose a different path. And I will take the blame for the route I chose and for the mistakes I've made. But when I look around, some of the people who actually took the same route I took are doing far worse than I am. They either didn't know somebody that knew somebody or simply just didn't kiss the right person's ass to get there. I never expected a handout myself. Yes, a little help would have been good, but I have taken the long route to get to where I'm at today. Although deep inside I would rather be doing other things, I know what's better for my life. And that's where I stand— confused and living a double life.

When I say that I'm living a confusing life, people don't actually see it until I admit my thoughts to them. In all reality, I only do what's legal because I know what's best for me and those around me, but there are many other things that I don't do right. I can preach to you on how to live or how to think, but behind the scenes I'm doing and thinking the complete opposite. It's only common sense. Think of where people get their best advice. Most of the time people who give advice are inspired either because of their own personal failures in life or from what they are still going through. Unfortunately, although I have been through many situations, I still continue to fall victim to most of the things I fell for when I was growing up.

I am addicted to all of the things that fascinated me when I was a teen and addicted to all of the wrong things that only I personally and selfishly enjoy. I really live my life how I want to live it. It doesn't matter what it involves. Not because I want to by choice, but because I really don't care about how people feel about me. It's selfish, but I want to be able to do whatever makes me happy. But when it comes to my personal life, I don't really care too much about other people's feelings, opinions, or even their advice. This is where I become frustrated and shut down. I know what's right and what's wrong just like I know legal from illegal. I just love the rush of doing what excites me. I do whatever makes me happy to momentarily take away the pain that I go through on daily basis. Unfortunately, there are people who begin to have feelings because they enjoy the time spent together instead of just enjoying things for the moment like I do.

When it comes to life as a whole, I see things completely the opposite. I try to do everything right but I just continue to hit walls every day. If it's not a money situation, it's a family situation. If it's not a work situation it's a personal problem. Then, if I choose to be quiet and ignore it, people think I don't care. So when I say fuck it and keep to myself and handle my issues how I want to, I'm fucked up. I never win. That's why I sometimes wish I had just continued living the life I did back when I really didn't care about shit. And I know that I need to think differently, but most of the time, people just drive me to that point. Here's how I look at it: My name is on my paycheck, so I spend my money how I want to. My name is on my bills, so I'm responsible to pay for them. My name is on my birth certificate, social security, and state ID, so I should be able to live my life however I choose to. If anyone feels any different, then maybe they should try to waste their time with someone else.

Getting older and wishing you could go back in time is something that everyone will eventually go through in life. But sooner or later you have to grow up and mature to realize that you just have to let the past be the past. It is something people have a very hard time letting go of. But if I have made it this far with what works for me, why should I change my ways only to make someone else's life happier? The last thing I want to do is sit back and be miserable because I made a choice to satisfy somebody else. One thing I do stay away from is telling people what to do or how to live. I wouldn't want anyone to get in the way of my choices or decisions. I feel that people should live their lives however they want to as long as there is no law against it. If you don't like what you see or hear, you have the choice to walk away. You should never let your feelings get the best of you. The last thing I want anyone saying is that they wasted their time with me when it was their choice to do so. Unless I intentionally mislead you, don't assume.

Part of me wants to be happy with doing what society considers the right thing to do. At the same time, I'm addicted to doing what many would consider wrong. I will honestly tell you that I have lived a double life since I began to do the complete opposite of what I was being raised to do. Everything that has ever presented itself to me as positive I have ruined somehow because I rarely ever saw the value or the future in it. The only effort I put into anything I did was just for that day only. I never thought about tomorrow and I damn sure didn't think further down the road. It just seems like the longer I live the harder my choices become. It's true when they tell you to enjoy life when you're young because time does fly. Most of my time goes on reminiscing on the past and wishing I could relive all my good moments.

As I got a little older, I went from living for the moment to taking it day by day. It was a start. Wherever I ended up I took it as if it was just meant to be. And that's with every choice I made. Life to me has been no different than having a relationship. The more I treated it like shit the more action I got out of it. Because every time I tried to do things the right way the results always came out wrong. Many will tell you that it is better to save the best for last. My best has already come and gone. I made the best life that I was capable of living and I have suffered both mentally and physically through the worst that I was able to deal with. Somehow, I'm still standing. Every day has been the same for many years now. I have become so accustomed to doing things the wrong way that no matter how many promises I make to change, nothing ever seems to make it past those words.

Although my intentions are never to hurt anyone, I live my life by only caring about what makes me happy. Now, that can be a really good thing or a very bad thing. My addiction is to make and enjoy the choices I want to in my life without worrying about what others think of me or about anything that I do. My advice to people is simple. Don't make the mistake of never voicing your opinions to people around you and then be pissed off at yourself later for allowing them to have some say in your life. If you don't want to be in any type of committed relationship or deal with a responsibility that's not yours, just stand up and say it. Set the boundaries with everything you do in life. Your life is yours. Live it how the fuck you want to live it.

To the rest of the world, many of the things that I say or do may or may not affect them in any way. I really just wanted to write this book because I know that there are a few members in my family and some friends that do wonder about me sometimes. I live a very personal life. In these past few years, I haven't really allowed many people into my life because I don't want to hear anyone complaining about how I live it. In some ways, you could say that I have become antisocial. In reality, I just love to mind my own business and keep people away from mine. I've learned the hard way that just knowing about someone else's business can get you caught up in so many different problems. But because I have distanced myself from so many people I grew up with, I feel like I have to explain my reasons why. I feel it's necessary for me to be able to move on, mentally and physically, with what's trapped inside of me.

The What If's

One thing we will never be able to know about life is what could have been. We can always guess at what would of or could have happened, but once things have already occurred, you will either end up wishing you could change the outcome or regretting that it occurred. I spend many days looking back into my past and wondering where I would be today had I not changed. It's crazy how when you are young and stupid the only future you ever thought about were the parties that weekend. I lost track of my future at such an early age that I'm still having a hard time getting back on track. I got so used to thinking that I wasn't going to make it past twenty-five that I never really prepared for my life properly. It was a joke to me when people used to tell me that I would regret wasting my time in the streets.

So, here I am today, admitting that I should have listened to those who attempted to change my ignorant ways. I adapted to a lifestyle that seemed to have had so many promises. Now that I look back, other than the lessons I learned, it was all a complete waste of time. The biggest reasons for my choices and becoming so rebellious was because whenever I looked around and compared my life to my friends' lives, I felt like my parents were too extreme and too strict compared to theirs. But where would I be today if I would have listened? I do wish I could go back. I wish I can make every kid out there in the world understand the value of advice from the adults they come across and consider it a blessing when someone takes time out of their life to help them look at theirs from another point of view. Who would really know better than someone who has already been through adult issues, worries, and struggles?

Weigh the situations you consider so tough to deal with and compare them to the worst-case scenario and I can guarantee you will appreciate life a little more than you do. I wish I knew how to weigh my options growing up. Nothing that I thought was important then would have even been a thought if I knew then what I know now. My first real adult decision was to kill for someone else just because I hung around them and dealt drugs together. You may ask why it would have been so simple to listen to a drug dealer in the streets tell me what to do than to listen to my parents? The answer back then was simple. I was getting from the streets what I couldn't get from my parents. Money, attention, and what I thought was respect. So I wonder today where I would be had we found the person we were looking to kill that day? Crazy how someone can put a gun in my hand to kill and go get locked up in a cell but hated my parents for giving me a curfew. How does that equal out in any way?

If I ever wanted to serve twenty years for shooting and killing people, I would have joined the military. That would have been the only situation that would have kept me away from my family, away from my friends, sleeping in the same room with other men and sharing bathrooms, but I would have taken pride in doing so. It's the only place I wouldn't mind being yelled at or being told what to do and when to do it by. But to be locked up in a prison for stupid shit? Fuck that. At least when a soldier says he has your back, he's not lying to you. In the streets, there is not one single person that truly means it when they tell you that they will die for you. If they do tell you that, they must have never experienced the feeling of a bullet going through them. With my own eyes, I saw a drug dealer who thought was the biggest thug in the streets lying on the ground crying after being grazed—yes, graze—by a fragment of a bullet on his leg. Not only did I find out he was not as tough as he claimed he was, I also found out that just being struck by a small part of a bullet does hurt.

In all reality, one should have a goal in life: to find out what you're really good at and use it to your advantage. Everything else will fall into place. Believe me, in this world, "you ain't shit" unless you are doing something productive and using your time wisely. If you think that the world is going to stop and take care of your struggles you are in for a big surprise. Especially if you're out there wasting most of your time doing illegal shit. I love it when I hear people call the street life "the struggle." The real struggle doesn't begin until you stop and look back and wonder how the hell you're going to survive being jobless or homeless. Because after a few years of being in and out of prison and realizing that no one will give you a job because of your record, or when your own family no longer tolerates your ignorant bullshit, where else do you really think you're going to end up? You shouldn't have to reach fifty and be looking back wishing you could do it all over again because you didn't take advantage of being young.

Life is more enjoyable when you surround yourself with positive people you can laugh with. Hanging out in places where you have to constantly keep your guards up and be watching your back or being pissed off wondering why someone is staring at you will only have you locked up in a cell or dead in a cemetery. It is obviously too late to wonder "what if" when you are buried in a cemetery, but how would you ever know what's on the other side if you don't give living a chance instead of putting your life on the line every second out in the streets? Yes, I do wonder where I would be today if I had continued hanging out on the streets. I even wonder where I would have been today had I listened to my parents and every other adult that I came across growing up. I understand that the life of crime may be an addiction to those that live it, but just like a drug addiction, the streets can and will kill you.

Life After Hustlin'

*S*ome people have wondered, while many others have
asked, how it was that I managed to begin selling
drugs by the age of twelve and continued through most
of my twenties without ever getting caught. The answer
is very simple; I just minded my own business. I made it
a hobby and not a career like most did. I followed all the
simple rules my dad had always taught me: never trust
anyone, never tell anyone your personal business, and
always think about the future. Of course, this advice was
given to me when he was yelling at me for misbehaving
in school, but it made a lot more sense when it came to
the streets. You can make money managing your own
business, you gain power by making your own choices
and decisions, and you will be respected for being true to

yourself while trying to be aware of your everyday surroundings. I guess you can say that was simple enough for me to do.

People don't really understand the aftereffects of being a drug dealer until they finally give it all up and look back at how much they have lost. One thing that really becomes hard to do is adjusting to the reality of life after the hustle. Everything that you're used to doing in the streets will be very hard to let go of once you begin to live a normal life. Because anyone that tells you that being in the streets is a normal way of living is one hundred percent confused. Anyone who claims to live it should be able to tell you this. It takes a certain kind of person to live the street life. Everything that is normal in a society does not apply to the streets. That's why people hold court on their own terms. This, many will deny, but in order to make it through the streets you have to be half real and half fake. Fake because you have to become a person who does not show fear and will do whatever it takes to keep others off you. Real, to me, means that you hide all real emotions and feeling in the fear that you will be judged a weak link.

Here's how I have come to this conclusion. I've hung around many individuals who have claimed to be real. And yes, at the time, it all seemed realistic to me that a person could and would do whatever means to prove their point. But fast forward to judgment day in the courtroom and their expressions were the complete opposite. I would be lying if I said I wasn't one of them. People think that just because a person sells drugs that they automatically should be considered street thugs. That's far from the reality. A person will sell drugs for many reasons, one of them being the obvious, which is to make money. The other two reasons, which many will probably try to deny, are that some people are just followers, while others do it for attention. The second two are the two biggest reasons why so many end up dead or locked up. There is your answer to being real or fake.

Take prison as an example. Not everyone is built for doing time. I'll be the first to tell you that I'm not...can I do prison time? Well, if I were sent there I would obviously have to. Would I be able to deal with it? Hell no. But because I chose to get in the game to make money instead of just wanting to be down with everyone else that was doing it, I remained focused on that one goal. A scared person will do almost anything to defend themselves; a wise person will think ahead first. Not only would

I have lost my freedom over something that had nothing to do with money, I could have also been killed. Those are two places where I obviously wouldn't be able to do what I needed to do to make money. I never really could put together why a person who claims that they are making money will constantly put themselves in a position to do the complete opposite of doing what they had to do to make money. It would be like going to work looking for a reason to get fired. It just doesn't make any sense.

Now that I am older, I can honestly tell you this: I don't have anything to show to you as proof that I was even out there, other than what a few people who knew about me could tell you. Another thing I can be honest enough to tell you are that none of my dreams of living off the money I made in the streets ever came true. I see how so many people make all these plans with money they haven't even made yet because they truly think that it's just that easy to do. Some do get lucky, but go too fast and you can lose it all in one shot. Me, I just did it when I felt I had to. Whenever I wanted anything I just went out, made the money for it, and was happy with being able to temporarily satisfy myself. These days, everyone wants to be known as "the man." But in the end, there could only be one man left standing, and that's the man that will bring you back to reality when he decides how much sleep time you will need in a cell to realize that it was all just a dream.

Let me honest before I go any further. I'm writing this book because I have been really fighting with myself about whether I should or shouldn't get back in it one more time. I guess I feel like I know now what I wish I'd known then. I feel like I have one shot left. I fight not to make that decision, but lately I have been physically putting myself in place while studying those who are doing it. It's tough, but I honestly don't think I'm going to fall back that far after making it this long without it. I guess you could say that it is a mental addiction, and I know I should never relapse.

In this book, I will take the time to show you how life after hustlin' has been for me. It hasn't been as easy as I thought it would be. The temptations of going back have always been there. The worry of making it without the fast money is scary. What scares me a little more than not being able to make the money I once did is getting caught now, after I got away with it for so many years. In a way, I sort of feel like the one soldier who made it back from a war. Everyone else is gone.

Deaf Ears

Many people wonder what it is they can do to stop crime or somehow try to slow it down. But before anyone can have any input on how to solve or control this issue, they must first try to find a way to better understand it. Many people jump to conclusions like blaming the parents, the environment, and even the system before taking a deeper look at the individual themselves and what motivates them to commit illegal incriminating acts. There are many excuses or reasons you can come up with to somehow try to figure out what triggers a person to lose their lives or freedom over what many consider foolish acts.

Many people don't think about their freedom until they have already lost it. But you can't regret something if you haven't been through it yet. So by the time an individual regrets their act and loses their freedom or life it is obviously already too late to go back. One of the biggest problems with the life of crime is that many times it all starts out as just fun. You test yourself daily to see what you can continue to get away with while the crimes you commit become worse and more dangerous. By the time you build your street credibility to the point of no return, you will continue to try to outdo yourself until you end up locked up or dead.

It's easy to point the finger and judge individuals who commit crimes, join gangs, or sell drugs. They are considered to being dangerous and unwanted in a normal society because what they do is not considered positive or productive. But whoever stops to ask them anything besides do they have an ID, do they have any drugs on them, or what gang do they belong to? To figure out the way a criminal in the streets thinks, you must first understand that they hate authority in every way. They may have already rebelled against their own parents, dropped out or been kicked out of school, and even have a criminal record. The only advice these people will listen to, even temporarily, will be from a judge in a courtroom.

At the same time, those who want things to change only unite once things have already occurred. They will form anti-violence groups, hold meetings at city council public safety committees, but just like a criminals regret is too late, so is the attempt to try to stop something they ignored or barely paid any attention to. It is normal to commit a crime in the projects or in any other drug infested areas of the streets. But when it happens anywhere else all of a sudden it is a concern. Most of the crimes these people discuss in meetings are usually held when a criminal goes outside of their environment and becomes a threat in places where crime is not expected to occur.

To be honest, there is no right or wrong way to handle this issue. In the streets, you will get praised for doing wrong and killed for trying to do the right thing. Crime is and will continue to occur no matter how many cops you have out there to protect us. Crime is not something that you can blame on anyone other than the person or people who are responsible for committing the acts. There are no boundaries once an individual has already chosen their target and made up their minds to commit a crime.

Here are some clues that may help you bring understanding to these individuals and where there may be headed. If a student barely gives any effort in doing well at school, he or she will more than likely give that same amount of effort in life. If they have dropped out because they hated school or because they were too lazy to wake up and go, how can you ever think or expect that they will want to work? If they become parents at an early age, understand that the only thing they can teach their children is what they know or what they are accustomed to doing. And if as adults these individuals are still thinking how they have always thought, why expect anything to change? In the end, the cycle will just continue.

So, who do you blame? *The Parents? The Environment? The System?* Or, do you just blame the individual themselves for their own acts? Those who are tired of crime in the streets want the cops to do their jobs but when they attempt to, they are criticized and accused of profiling or abusing their power. When criminals are locked up, they are given bonds to get out within hours. So when is crime going to be taken seriously? Is there a need for a bond so that the criminal while awaiting his court appearance is out committing other crimes he or she may get away with? Is there a need to continue to grant someone their freedom when they don't have a high school diploma, ever had a job, or even the motivation to doing the right things in life? I understand and also agree that there are certain people that need a second or maybe even a third chance. But when is enough enough? Is it when you can finally put someone away for the rest of their life? By then, someone is dead while both sides of the family have to grieve forever.

Stress to Impress

$\mathscr{P}$ick a person you would want to be like and I will show you a person who spends twice the amount of time trying to impress others as you would trying to be like them. Role models feed off the attention they create. Many people think that what they see in the light is the same exact person they will see in the dark. Nothing is ever what it seems. If you think that a role model lives a positive life round the clock seven days a week you are definitely confused. As far as I'm concerned, role models don't do anything for free. If an individual is not being paid somehow to be the person others want them to act like, you will definitely see the person they truly are behind closed doors. If you were ever able to get behind those closed doors and see the real person behind the role model, you will see that he or she may be no different than anyone else. Then you have the nobodies who live their lives trying to be somebody by doing anything just to be noticed.

You ever dated the one you thought was the one meant for you to be with for the rest of your life? Well it's kind of the same thing. Everything that person does will impress you and you actually begin to feel like it's going to be like that forever. When you begin to see the real person behind what you used to be impressed by, you will see that they are human just like you. If you are constantly looking up to someone, it is obviously because they make you feel like you are under them. Here's what I consider a role model. I think that people who really don't care about how other's feel about them are the realest people you can surround yourself with. In my opinion, no one should ever feel like they have to do anything for people who wouldn't care about them if they didn't have something for others to judge them by. Take away the fame or the fortune and you end up with the real person behind the face you think you know.

It's called an out-of-body experience because you yourself can't believe that you are being accepted in ways you never expected to be. Then you keep fighting to get that rush each and every time you step foot in public to try and outdo yourself. Eventually, you become your own worst enemy because you fight mentally and physically only to impress others. When the public sees that other side of you, you will no longer be the person they always praised. Once you show people that you make mistakes or make bad choices, too, they will notice you are just like them. The sad part about it is the obvious part. You always were human. You were only being judged in the light. Not in your darkest moments. Stars shine in the dark because in the light everything is hidden.

My role models lived for the moment. But those moments became a lifetime of memories. The role models I learned from are no longer here. I actually learned more from their failures than I did from the many positive things I should have paid attention to. Do I ever think there were people who wanted to be like me? I don't know. In reality, I always wanted to know who wanted me dead and why? That would have given me a clear implication of how others may have perceived me in public do to my actions in the streets. Not only does negativity sell, it also brings many unwanted and unexpected problems. And I know that I did many things that may have offended many people. I think its funny how when you just say or do things just to accommodate others how easily you are accepted. But if you stated how you truly felt or did what you really wanted to do many would be offended by it. I know there are people who probably stood next to me and just stared because they hated looking at who or what they thought I was. Because if they ever really got to know the real me they would have always been wrong in how they judged me.

These days, without a witness to testify the only person that believes the actual truth is the person telling the story. In other words, if a person came out and really expressed how they truly felt deep inside chances were they would no longer be treated the same. Truthfully, I like realness in a person. I don't like when a person expresses their opinions as if they are facts. Then you have those who never seem to give a person a chance to explain their way of thinking without being judged first. Many of the people who claimed to have disliked me were only going by what other people have said about me that they probably heard themselves. Behind closed doors, I am the same person I am in public. I think and state how I feel and I do what I want. Don't get me wrong, there are times when I may not express myself because I fear no one will understand. But I will never do something I didn't want to just to be accepted.

If people don't expect others to judge them by their actions then why should we judge an actor on their acting? Behind the actor there is a person. So why should I act a certain way only to entertain people? Not everything in life is meant for everyone. There are things in life that only a few people can handle under pressure. What works for one person definitely may not work for others. Yes we are all humans. But not everyone can hit a curve ball or be quick on their feet. Who is anyone else to tell you what they feel is best for you? Some people love things you may hate. But if it works for them who are we to tell them what's better? Whatever happened to living how you want to live? I can understand advice. But to judge someone you see every day? Someone who is constantly doing the same things they seem to enjoy? That's really none of our business to try to change.

Without sounding conceited, I think that the people who have always judged me were those who had less than me or wanted what I had. Honestly though, nothing I have ever done in my life was intentionally done to offend anyone. I have always done what made me happy. I think

I'm perfect. I think all people are perfect. Perfect in their own way to do whatever makes them happy. If they didn't like what they did then they wouldn't be doing it. Fuck what everyone else thinks. How everyone else thinks or feels should be irrelevant. Chances are people will only have good things to say about you when you are dead and gone. Because as long as you are alive, everyone feels they can judge you like their lives are perfect next to yours. So I think that it is perfectly fine for people to live how they want. If it offends others than maybe others are paying too close attention to things that shouldn't concern them. But if a person chose to just impress others only to be accepted than they were only setting themselves up to be judged when the truth comes out. I'm no role model; I'm far from it. One thing I can't do is live a lie.

Handout

Many people think they have an idea of what it is like to suffer by basing their own personal situations of the past and comparing it to their present life or by seeing certain similarities in what others around them may be going through. But to be truthful, not only do people deal with certain matters differently, it also affects them differently. No one personally feels what an individual goes through in their worst moments like the individual themselves does. Many will claim that they have suffered so much that they feel they have become immune to pain, but even then, each and every new experience carries its own weight. Some may be stronger in dealing with personal issues while others carry it with a heavy guilty burden and wish daily they could turn back the hands of time to have the outcome be less tragic or painful. The thought of things happening for a reason has become the only answer to all of the unexplainable situations many have been a witness to or have been personally involved in dealing with.

Feelings though, let's face it. We may get a little emotional over things that may occur around us or on the news, but nothing comes close to the feeling of when it hits home. It's one thing to be a witness, but it's another thing to be the suspect or the victim. Likewise, it's one thing to be free and another to be locked up or dead. This is the reason why I think before I speak and before I react all the time. We can say everything we will do when put in certain situations but once you end up on the receiving end, the thoughts and feelings of it all become mostly regrets. I believe that most of the negative situations we face in life come with warning signs and could also be avoided if we paid more attention. There is a big difference between a mistake and a choice. Mistakes happen. Choices are made.

No matter what occurs in our lives, we feel, somehow, that it has its purpose. What's meant to occur has already been assigned its destiny. The outcome of all movement on earth has been pre-arranged by its own creator. Unfortunately there will always be the chosen ones that will have to wake up to the unexpected bad news. It's a random act of the unexpected that goes around finding the next victims turns to have to deal with the unfortunate situations that were meant to occur. It's kind of like trying to out run from your own shadow. These situations will follow you until the time of occurrence expires without warning. It's like a bomb that goes off without you ever knowing it had been there ticking.

Seriously though, what is not part of life? Every time I turn around there is someone either saying "it's part of life" or "that it was meant to be." No shit. If it happens then it is very obvious to me that it is part of life. Even if it was a mistake or accident, it's part of life. If you can see it, smell it, touch it, feel it — physically or mentally — it is a part of life. You just have to find the best way to deal with it. It kills me when people say that there are certain things that aren't supposed to happen when it's something negative but when it's something positive that occurs they can't believe it. If anything that happens on a playing field is part of the game than anything that happens to you or around you is part of your life.

The only time it shouldn't be a part of your life is when it is none of your business. But even then you can still learn some things from it.

I, myself, should have been a janitor. I say that because it seems like every day I wake up, I'm just cleaning up everyone's shit like I'm the one who made the mess. The majority of my issues aren't even my own. All of my stress comes from people that call me with their problems and ask me for advice, then call me insensitive when I tell them how I truly feel. Like money is the root of all evil, assholes are the root of all the shit I have to deal with. You know what bothers me the most? It's the people who I have already given advice to but didn't agree with what I told them to do and decided to take their own route. Just like I hate it when I have to tell people "I told you so." I hate it just as much when they say to me, "I should have listened." Doesn't that sound like you've both wasted your time with each other?

Sit there quietly for a few minutes and listen to the clock tick. If you feel like you can be making better use of your time, it's because you probably should. Here is my advice: get up off your ass and go at least attempt to do something that will make your life better. Sitting around bitching all day and blaming other people for the problems that you created is not an excuse, reason, or solution to anything. I'll put it to you this way; no one loses any sleep or wakes up thinking of ways to help you fix your problems unless they are being paid for it. In other words, no one really cares unless they benefit from your failure somehow. It's even beneficial to some people to just to rub it in your face first that they were right and you were wrong before they offer helping you. Because these days, even advice has a price, nothing is free.

To me, the easiest things to deal with are the situations I can't do anything about. If I can't fix it or change it, what's the point in wasting my time dealing with it? The only thing I can do is try my hardest to never repeat being in the same situation again. It's the little things that bother me. Let me clarify what I'm saying. If it was left up to someone else to decide where you ended up, what the fuck can I do to save you? These are the types of people I'm talking about. Women who have kids with deadbeat dads who don't give them money or are locked up. People who are locked up or have cases pending. People who are broke because they spent all their money on stupid shit. People who are on the run over some dumb shit. People who are in a fucked up relationship and claim they can't get out. People who are constantly in the middle of some shit because they can't mind their own business. If you are one of these types of people, here are some things you can do. Mind your own fucking business, move the fuck on, and stop bitching all day. No one should have any control over you or any choice you make. And if you are already in a messed up situation, find a way to get out of it and stay as far away as possible.

Yes, I do understand that mistakes occur. But when things happen to someone you've been warning day in and day out, you tend to just give up on them. Then, when you give up on them, they get pissed off because they feel you don't care enough to help them get out of the situation they are in. When they end up with a criminal record, they can't find a job. When they are broke, they ask to borrow money. When they are in prison, they need a visit. When they don't have a car, they ask you for a ride. When they can't find a solution to their issues, they call you for advice. It wasn't until they had their backs up against the wall with nowhere to run and hide that they would actually stop and take the time to listen.

Eventually they had to somehow try to understand that the advice being given to them was to prevent negative things from happening. But like most that chose not to listen, they had to learn the hard way after!

People say I'm crazy because I'm always assuming the worse or over analyzing all the time. Think about this though. People drive to and from work all the time and never think of getting in an accident, right? People fly planes everyday picturing already landing and having a great vacation before they even take off. People drive over bridges all the time and never think they can collapse. But can something crazy happen without warning? Of course they can. But even though they are part of life, they are called accidents. Not choices. If you can control it somehow, you have options. If you have a million choices, you can decide. The problem with so many people these days is that they never think that it can happen to them. It has always been easier for people to point the finger than to use their own common sense. But when it does happen to them, they either adapt to the situation and stay stuck or simply just give up. And try giving advice to those kinds of people and see how far you can get. I can't be like that. That shit scares me. Failure is not a choice, option, or a solution for me.

It's not so much that I live in fear every day or that I'm always thinking about the worse things. I'm just cautious of everything that I do. I always think about the worst possible thing that could happen before I commit to doing anything. Back in the day, you could have put me in any situation and I can honestly tell you that I did not give a fuck about how to deal with it. If I had to fight over it I would have. If I had to take, rob or steal I would have. Pride and ego has more power over you than you have over your own choices. These days I would rather take the long route to end up on the other side. You learn to appreciate everything in life a lot more when you don't take short cuts. But you know what motivates me to get the things I want in life? Fear does. I fear failure more than anything else in life. I fear anything that has to deal with me having to ask for help or a favor. The only people that should be helping me if I can't help myself are doctors at a hospital. Not a psychiatrist, not welfare, not a counselor, and definitely not a police officer or judge in a courtroom.

I don't depend on anybody, so I feel that no one should rely on me to get them out of situations they get themselves into. There are many people in my life today that seem to feel that it is my responsibility to fix everything they go through. Yes, it is unfortunate that people have to go through rough times. But it's part of life. Everyone has to experience pain in their lives sometimes. It's all up to them whether they learn from it or not. So ask yourself, is everything you go through part of life? Or do you feel like it's a matter of being unlucky or cursed? Because if it's about luck, I can tell you that I might not be the person to turn to for advice. I don't rely on luck or wishes. I just live. Whatever happens just happens. What I am today is obvious that it was meant to be. I cannot go the rest of my life wishing things were different. When I go through my moments in life I just shut down, disappear, and deal with it without involving anyone else. Why should two of us deal with one matter? Life is hard enough for one person. Why involve others?

I love to share. If I have enough to give away, I will. But before I do that, I will try to teach you how to earn things on your own just like I was taught. I don't just give handouts. If you show me that you are trying I will do my best to give you a hand. If you don't listen to my advice then I would put you out of my life. That's what I call a hand out. But how can you expect for me to give you things that I also have to work hard to get myself? You don't think I need things too? That doesn't make any sense to me. Would you do the same for me? And if your answer is yes then try to prove it to me. If your answer is no then why should I? The people who have it made in life have the same things to lose that you as a failure want to gain. So why would anyone want to switch sides? Why would you feel that because you are struggling in life that people need or have to give you money, give you a ride or a place to live for free? Isn't that embarrassing to you? Sounds like prison may be the only place where you can get all three without having to beg.

I do understand people may need help sometimes. But if helping others fucks you up or gets you in trouble somehow, then you don't need them in your life. I don't love misery and I definitely hate bad company. Here's how you become rich in life. My dad always told me that a friend was like a dollar in my pocket. And I'm broke so what should that tell you? I may not be able to save my money but I damn sure not going to waste my time. I've wasted more than enough time in my own life doing things I thought were worth it and knew I needed to change. So I no longer pay people attention when they come crying to me about their struggles. In other words, save your breath and stop wasting your time by paying attention to people who are not going to change. They say that time is money. Why should anyone else be wasting yours?

Lock and Key

The older I get, the wiser I feel my decisions have been. Compared to the many people I have come across who's biggest fears have been to never find the "right one," I think I will continue being even more patient when I hear them complaining and wishing they were in my shoes. I never cared about what people felt or thought was right just because it's considered politically correct or because society expects you to live according to certain standards. First of all, society isn't helping me pay my bills. My significant other should be. And as far as being politically correct? Fuck that, too. Everyone's situation is different. All I have ever wanted was someone to be at least half responsible enough to deal with their own responsibilities. I have always been willing to meet them half way with bills and anything else I could help out with. All the people I have dealt with seem to always be worry more about spending time together then spending their money wisely. They buy everything they want and when the bills come at the end of the month they act like an unknown company is suing them. The older I got, the more I began to feel like a relationship was more than just having a beautiful woman. To me, if you weren't in it to also prepare for the future, what's the point?

I remember back when I was single and had no kids and listening to all of the couples that I thought would have been happily together forever. Man did they leave me confused. They either ended up co-parenting or not even in their kids' lives at all. That had always been my biggest fear. I never wanted to end up being that dad who would be away from the kids, never mind having some other man raising them. When I would ask them why they did get married and had kids in return all I heard was complaints. Most say that they wish they would have been more patient and had enjoyed their lives a bit more before becoming involved in such a big commitment they hardly ever prepared for. Most of the people I knew were only together because of looks. It was rare that you found a couple that stayed together as a family and lived in the same home.

You sometimes have to ask yourself this question. Is life about living comfortably or is it about living better than others? Because if you look deep into the reasons why people struggle so much it is usually because aside from taking care of their responsibilities they tend to almost want to compete with others by making their appearance to the world a priority. It's like trying to impress a judge by wearing a suit and tie only when it comes to facing time in a courtroom. Only in this case people are worried about being judged by their peers. I understand that people want to look and feel good. But people should also understand that there is going to be a time where you have to decide on things that are just wants compared to those that are needs. I remember those days when I used to think my appearance in front of others was such a big deal for me. All until I was almost went broke and barely had enough money for my bills. Trust and believe that I fully understand the struggle between wanting to look good in public and also trying to keep up with responsibilities as an adult. You can continue trying to please the world all you want, but in the end, your main priorities should always come first.

Everyone struggles sometimes. But my struggles weren't by choice. It was because I actually took care of all my priorities and didn't really care about not having extra money to enjoy. But when it came to relationships, most of the situations I had to deal with were all backwards. Most of the women of my past seemed more like they wanted to be taken care of more than they were building for a future together. And that has always been the reason why I have always had an issue with staying together. It's great to go out and have a good time every once in a while, but going broke over them was not part of the plan.

I'm nobody's "Sugar Daddy" or Fucking Hero. That's a role that some men played until they got what they wanted or felt there was nothing left for them to continue chasing after. Men can also be just as bad as women if not worse. They would continue to spend until they went broke if they were at least getting something in return for it. In most cases, they weren't looking to be or fall in love. If you had your own place and a car, that was like jack pot to most of them. As for me, I always had both so there was no need to have to use anyone for those things. But I can assure you of one thing. Lose any of those two things and I can guarantee you that you will slowly begin to see them a lot less as time went by. These were the types of situations that people got so used to that when they actually found someone better than what they had been dealing with; they didn't know how to adapt to better things. And not having your responsibilities being your priority has always been my biggest turn off.

I was just as afraid to be in a relationship as I was to leave the street life. I was afraid I would no longer be in control of my own actions. Like I said, I hated answering to anyone. I never liked explaining myself. Never mind being around someone who was going to cry because I didn't answer my phone one night or go hysterical because I wasn't being romantic enough. Where I come from there was no such thing as enough. But it had nothing to do with being romantic. You could never have enough girls, money, cars, guns, respect, and most importantly, you had a sense power. And there was more than enough to go around. So to settle for one or one thing was far from anyone's thoughts or goal. Everything in the street life is exaggerated. Why do you think I had so much fun? If one thing didn't work we always had other options. Think of it this way. People are in prison for these same reasons I have just mentioned. They are in prison because when it came to money, power, and respect, they just couldn't get enough of it. The worse that could have happened was being killed. And many were willing to take that risk. But when it came to relationships, now you know why there are so many fatherless kids running around out there. It wasn't from being romantically in love. It was because they had more than enough to pick from. I will admit this: most men might be dogs. Unfortunately, most women are insecure and never satisfied.

Always remember this. You should never feel like you have to just give in just to make someone happy. Once you are in a relationship, it is no longer about who is right or who is wrong. It's about being happy together. If you can't be happy together, then you should not keep trying to right the unfixable wrongs until you both end up hating or wanting to kill each other. You do have the choice of what type of relationships you want to be in. You can be in a lock and key relationship where one is meant for the other. Or you can be in a ball and chain relationship where you feel like you have to ask permission to do what a normal adult should be able to do without asking.

Butterflies

Sometimes, I feel like I am stuck being unlucky or confused. I wonder if things do happen for a reason that I just have to accept without really understanding why they occur. I have been told that I will never know outcome unless I try when it came to things I never gave enough effort to. People have always told me to expand my horizons in life and get out of my everyday routines. And I can admit that I have been stuck in the same routines because I feel like if I did something else I would suffer consequences I have dodged all my life. It's like when people say, "Why fix things that aren't broken?" It's the complete opposite for me. Those who can see right through me always say I am broken up inside and need to fix things in order to be happy. In most cases, they are right. It is true. I have held on to so many things in my life

I should have already let go of. I'm like a pack rat when it comes to holding on to things from the past.

I'm the kind of person who always seems to have all the right answers to everyone else's issues but never could fix my own. I know what I have to do to make things better but I guess I haven't been able to find the right people to do it with. If there were one person who would be able to prove that opposites attract, it wouldn't be me. I'm the lucky one who always seems to run into the same types of people who either have similar issues as I do or far worse. What's sad is that I have become so accustomed to suffering that I have accepted it as what was meant for me. But in many cases, it has made me stronger, too. To me, love has become more of a risk than a dream. What's growth when it involves only caring until the love is gone?

Many people want to experience happiness, but most are afraid of commitment in fear that they will no longer be able to have fun. Fun in a sense of being able to do whatever they want to do without having any strings attached to then explaining themselves or fearing that they would have to answer to someone for their actions. This is completely understandable. But there comes a time when we will experience so many missed opportunities we will look back and feel regret. They say that opportunity always knocks at your door. Unfortunately, when you have more than one option knocking, it gives you more choices to choose from. Once everything becomes a choice you run a greater risk of making the wrong decision because everything looks worth choosing from. Unfortunately, most of our choices are made out of desperation and curiosity rather than for what's best for us. We always think that no matter what choices we make, we could always go back and change it all by trying to figure out where we went wrong in the first place. But we must always keep in mind that while a person takes their time to make their decisions, other people are also trying to figure out what's best for them as well.

One of the reasons why I have always avoided being in a committed relationship is because I always felt like I was going to be missing out on something better. We always seem to want more than what we already have rather than comparing it to what it could be. We do it financially, materialistically, and we even do it with people who we should be satisfied with having in our lives. No matter how much money we have, we always want more instead of remembering the times we didn't have shit. If

I met somebody that I thought was worth being with, I always ended up running into someone else who seems could also be the one. No matter how much of anything I have, everything always seems to get old. So, staying committed to just one person or a thing has obviously not been easy for me.

Regret is something that most of us will experience when it comes to breaking up. We will either regret leaving someone and wishing we would have stayed together and worked things out or regret that you stayed too long when you should have left sooner. But if unconditional love is falling in love all over and over again more and more each day when you see or think about the person, then how much love will you have in the end when you both can no longer see eye to eye? It's true, you can be the world's most famous icon or the world's richest person, but without love you'll always have an empty feeling. I've been looking forward to meeting the person that will take my breath away. And many times, it has only occurred during the honeymoon stages. These days though, it seems like people have either too much baggage or never take the time to adjust to one another. It's almost like a continuance of a previous relationship that went wrong and it was never their fault. Sometimes you have to look in the mirror and understand that an approach you take with certain people isn't always going to work with someone new. Yes, you can learn from the past. But if you carry it into another relationship you can or will end up right back to where you started, by yourself.

My advice to anyone dealing with somebody who is confused is to never allow anyone to make you a choice. Because even when they choose you they will always be wondering in their thoughts what things would have been like had they made the opposite choice. Then when you try to leave them they seem to do everything in their power to keep you close. They do things that they should have been doing in the first place to make things work. But it's not until you begin to talk about going separate ways that all of a sudden they want you and don't want to lose you. Now that's confusing. Dysfunctional if you ask me. But I've been there so I can laugh about it, too.

Here is an example of one of the reasons why I really never cared so much about being in a relationship or falling in love. Relationships always start out the same way. Everything is good in the beginning. Of course, no one is going to show you their true colors from the start.

It's even worse when they come out and tell you what they expect from you and you haven't even been in the situation yet. Those were the signs telling me that they have been through many rough times in previous relationships. But I don't want to hear about things they expect from me. I should be the judge in how to respond to certain things they deserve or not. You can't just sit around and expect to be treated a certain way if you're not going to put in the work. So now when things don't work out, all of a sudden I'm no different than the people they have dealt with in the past. I know that no relationship is perfect, but I'm not going to waste my time arguing or fighting with someone over and over again about the same issues.

The only thing I would fight with is my own thoughts trying to decide whether I want to deal with the bullshit or not. Honestly, what is real love when the love is easily replaced by hate when it's no longer there? Some may say that it is better to experience love and lose it rather than never experience it. That, to me, is like winning the lotto and ending up being more broke than you were before you bought the ticket. Love is supposed to be life's greatest gift, right? ...But picture being given a gift one day, then later having someone take it back from you. I've had butterflies in my stomach before—only to see them fly away. I think my problem is that I put too much pressure on a person to plan for the future instead of just focusing on being romantic. Because what's the point in being in a relationship if you're not focusing on the future as well? Relationships will never work if a person's responsibilities and priorities aren't where they should be.

Moving on is usually the hardest part of a relationship. In the end, you feel like you put so much effort into it for nothing, just to start all over again with somebody else. You should always do whatever it takes for you to be happy, but only if the other person is willing to change in order to make it work. You should never worry about how stupid you look to everyone else. Everyone has to go through rough times to make certain things work out. Chances are that the more you go through, the closer you will become. Relationships aren't made from giving it a title just because you're partners. It takes building together to make a stronger bond. The only thing it all depends on is how much you want to put up with. I've become a little more patient these days. I tolerate a lot more than I used to in the past. But when I feel like I'm being played with, I have to make the choice on how long I'm willing to wait.

In order for me to be patient and continue on, there have to be signs of improvement.

There is more to me than the tough exterior, but my heart has hardened. People may think I don't embrace love because it's a sign of being weak, but that's not the case. My biggest problem with love is that I go into a relationship already expecting the worse. I've had so many negative experiences with it in the past because I try to focus on priorities first. While my partner concentrates on just being romantic, I concentrate more on trying to mold them to think about the future. I never really take the time to actually think that they might have had other negative experiences as well. But how long do I have to wait when it comes to being patient? Or how many times do we really have to go through the same things before there is understanding? I have felt like I have been more of a coach than I have been someone's partner in a relationship. People seem to get embarrassed or take things personal when they're being guided to correct certain things about themselves instead of looking at it as compromising.

Will I ever love someone or commit myself to a faithful relationship? Of course I will. I'm ready to do that now. But I'm not going to settle with just anyone because I'm alone. I find myself thinking about some of my missed opportunities when I let go or messed up. Those were learning experiences that I will try to never repeat. These days, I am willing to not only meet a person halfway but also give them my all. I'm more focused now than when I was growing up. I don't want to have more than one option. That has been nothing but a headache for me. I want to share my life with someone who is as willing to learn me and adjust to me as I am willing to do for them.

Witnesses

*I*f you constantly meet people halfway, you will forever breakeven—or end up losing. I know that life shouldn't always be about winning or losing, but you should at least benefit somehow without always being taken advantage of. There are many people around you with angles you will never be able to figure out because in front of you they will act and go right along with you as long as they have something to gain. All you have to do is learn how to say no to them once in a while and you will see exactly what kinds of people you are surrounded by. Because if you really think about it, most people stay friends for many years holding back things about each other only to keep the friendship. The moment you try to express how you truly feel about something, you become enemies overnight. It's almost like you have to hold back true feelings while putting a smile on your face to keep from opening up. These days though, it's difficult to keep friends around. I was always told to speak my mind if I ever had an issue. The moment I began doing it, people were quickly getting offended. When I began noticing that, I came up with one solution. Fuck friends.

Want to know the truth about friends, some of them ain't shit. Better yet, most of them ain't shit. I've realized that just because a friend of mine introduces me to a friend of theirs does not make us all best friends. That's a mistake most of us make in life. Then we're stuck wondering how it is that everyone knows our business. Why it is that people never seem to ask the most important question when it comes to arguing or fighting, which is who started it in the first place. I mean, in all reality, who knows all your personal business to begin with? Do you really trust a close friend that much? That you think someone mysteriously figured out all your secrets? Are we really that stupid? You know what a friend has become for me in my life? One more witness to run their mouth about my personal business. They run their mouth so much that I've even made up lies that have come back to me. I'll explain the reason why people run their mouths so much. One, they love to spread new news. They want to be the first to claim they knew about something. And two, they love problems. They want to see people argue or fight.

I've made it through my entire adult life by keeping to myself, minding my own business and knowing how to pick my battles. People around me were constantly losing their freedom and lives over those three things at a very fast rate. I never wanted to be like or end up like any of them. Although I express myself through writing, I never become the vocal advocate in public trying to change things or force people to understand my view and turning everything into a debate. First off, if you just mind your own business, no one would ever be in yours. You will never be a target. And secondly, if you just keep to yourself, no one would ever know too much about your personal business and spread rumors about you. People should only know what you think they should. There are no such things as secrets in this world. As far as picking my battles, it was all about common sense. I'm no idiot. I never felt the need to have to react to everyone's igno-rance even when they tried to push me. For all I knew, I was probably being set up just for the kill.

As a teen, I would spend many days pissed off and ready to fight because I could never figure out how people knew all of my business all the time. It took me many years to realize that I had way too many people in my life I really thought I could trust. My own friends have told on me more than any criminal in the street ever has. How backwards is that? But when you know a lot of people that you think you can trust you tend to share more with them than you should. Just because a person laughs and smiles, you really think you can rely on them to never betray you in any way. And to me, most were clowns. You know deep inside that you have changed any time you begin a sentence with, "five years ago I would have," when it comes to how you react to certain things. I found myself saying that at least three times a week over bullshit. You've reached a sad moment in your life when it's your friends who begin to look like the real enemies. I'm not just talking about friends in the streets; I'm also talking about friends I grew up with.

One thing I always had an issue with was gossip. I hated it so much because I knew that when it was about me, it was the ones I trusted most who were starting it all. One would think it was out of jealousy but in most cases they just couldn't keep their mouths shut. Think of it this way. If you trust your closest friend and something you only told them gets back to you, where's the trust? How can you ever trust a friend when he or she can't keep a secret? Well, the answer is simple. Everyone has a friend they think they can trust. I just think it's funny how when people spread rumors about someone the first thing they say is, "You didn't hear it from me." And I'm thinking to myself, how the fuck can I ever trust you when you're gossiping about someone else to me?

A negative that actually proved positive for me is when people say that good guys always finish last. And that's how I always felt. Even when I thought I was doing not only what I thought was right, but also what I felt was best. With the exception of my parents and my brothers, I never really paid any attention to anything outside of that. Even when it came to my family, I chose to be the different one. I was the first one out of all of us who began to reach out to the streets to solve my personal problems. I take full responsibility for the reasons why some of my brothers ended up on the wrong side of the law. I never meant for things to get out of control like they did. My intentions were to try to hide what I was going through in my personal life by choosing the streets to rebel against everything and everyone who didn't understand me. The street life is the only place where you could not only do no wrong but also meet people who were living by their own rules. The only difference was that I was rebelling against house rules. Most of the people I hung around were born and raised right into it.

Unfortunately, I ended up loving it. I felt free. Everyone seemed to agree with all of my views. Especially when they were all negative. I began to feel closer to "my boys" in the streets than my own family. No matter what I wanted or needed, they had it. If they didn't have it, we made it happen. Everything worked quickly. Time was all we had. In comparison to a prison, the only difference was that bars and cells didn't surround the projects. Like an inmate in prison, all we ever did was tell stories and waste time all day. But for the time being, it was those conversations that made me feel like I was part of something. Till this day, I'm still trying to figure out what I was a part of; because in the end, no one really wins. You can hang out with all your boys and call it a crew or a gang, but at the end of the day, it's really every man for himself.

Lucky for me, I'm still alive to tell you that there is really nothing like your real family. You may not be able to get along with most of them, but they're not looking to kill you like many of the people I hung around with did.

When they tell you that criminals in the streets live like crabs in a bucket, they mean just that. Because you can always work your way to the top and feel like you have accomplished something. But where do you go from there? Once you realize you really haven't accomplished anything, you will be left trying to claw your way back into a normal society. And if all you really know about is the street life, where do you think it's going to be that easy for you to fit in? Do you really think there is a place for you to work at where you can act, speak, and look like a criminal and make it in normal society? The only two things you can probably become besides dead or locked up is an athlete or rapper. Other than that, it will be very hard dealing with people who won't understand you, but at the same time don't want to deal with you either. I mean, if you didn't get along with others in the streets who you did have something in common with, how the hell do you think you're ever going to get along with people who don't?

On that note, I really feel like I have to say this. I don't care who your favorite rapper is or what your favorite song is. Understand one thing: you will never be them. You can end up being like the victims they may talk about, but you will never be them. You can rap along and dance to any song you want. You can walk and talk like them all you want. But always remember, you will never ever be them. Stop living your life thinking you're the person they are talking about. I don't care if you are in the arena singing along to their songs. They don't know you. If you are willing to die or kill because a song made you do it, then you're an idiot. You can love the music and appreciate it for the art, but you are not and never will be them. I just felt like I really had to say that.

One thing that I am not going to agree with is when people who hangout in the streets claim that they are a product of their environment. The real truth is they are an example of it. It was a choice. It was not mandatory. And I lost many good years in search of something many people have been killed over. It was all an illusion, a dream that turned into a nightmare. I chose to take a different route because I thought I was man enough to do things my way. Lucky for me, I made it out without a scratch. When your closest ones try to keep you in line and it begins to feel more like a punishment instead of motivation, we can agree on one thing. There is no harder punishment to deal with than the one you chose to get into on your own. Because the only lesson you can really learn from a consequence is to never repeat the act again. You can choose your friends over family all you want. But where do you think you're going to end up when all of you want the same things. Not one man in this world wants to finish second. Never mind being dead or locked up. You really think they are going to take your place when they face those consequences?

For most of my life, I have felt like the people I consider close to be have used me. They've stolen and continued to take and in the end I realized they were all being disloyal to me. But understand this: a lonely life without issues is a boring life to live, but a lonely life without fake friends and family is the one I would rather live. Today, I am blind to those I don't want to see and deaf to the ones I don't want to hear. Many have come and many have gone, most really weren't worth keeping around. I would rather it be that way than to deal with bullshit one more day. In no other shape or form, would I want it any other way. Easy to think we all know each other when there is always something new to learn. Nothing else for me to learn though, I taught myself never to trust or even waste time with people who aren't worth being real to anymore. Cause unkindly in return, people only judge you by the weakness they take advantage of. Friendship is based on loyalty and honesty. Unfortunately for me it was always one sided while they showed me two faces that I was confused to pick from. Put it this way, the less I know the better. This way no one could ever come to me and either ask me anything or accuse me of being involved somehow.

I've realized that by trying to live a perfect life you tend to screw up more than when you just live it. Even when you think that you're making the right choices and decisions things don't always necessarily go your way. Those who speak negative of me while I'm still here will hopefully change their minds when I'm gone. I would hope that they would just remember the good things I have done and and hopefully just learn from my mistakes. I'm human just like everyone else. Everyone makes mistakes and bad choices. I've always kept it in the back of my thoughts that anything that I say or do can be misunderstood in the minds of others or misinterpreted through their opinions. But I also understand that not everyone thinks the same way. Maybe when I'm gone people will realize what I was worth. Because truthfully, many people who I thought were worth anything to me made me feel worthless. It's unfortunate and sad because all I ever expected in return for giving them a part of me was a true friendship. Remember this: friends don't ask if you want help, they just do it. Anyone who asks if you want help may not actually want to. But it should never be a choice for someone who acts like they really care; they shouldn't even feel the need to ask.

I've tried loving life and appreciating people without taking it or them for granted. But it's like something always forces me to make choices and decisions that only seem to make matters worse. No matter what questions I've asked, it always seemed like all I ever got in return were all the wrong answers. People say that life has given to me in return what was meant. That could be true. But I've always felt like I have deserved much more. You can only hope to get back at least some of what you've put into it. In most cases, though, that's not true. If you do things in life expecting the same in return, chances are you will be very disappointed. If you are comfortable and happy with yourself, then there is no need to change the people, places, or the things you have. That's never been the case in my life though. Not to say that I have always been right.

It has just been very difficult for people to understand me. At the end of the day all that I have ever asked for was that people treated me like I always treated them. I hate show offs and I hate fake people. Respect goes both ways. If you are "Fake" toward me, understand that I can easily figure you out. I've been around it for most of my life. No one should ever have to feel like they have to waste their time around me. I love being by myself. There is nothing more peaceful.

One thing that I really understand about life is that everything not only happens for a reason but that you should never go backwards in life unless you are trying to remind yourself of something you never want to experience again. What I am basically saying is that your past should never be better than your future. Everyone is dealt a hand to play with, but it's how you play and who you play with or against that determines how long the game will last. The truth offends some while lies mislead others. Life is like chasing a dream full of nightmares in between. One minute, life gives you happiness, and then it takes it all back as if you never deserved it. Although at times we may feel like we don't understand it or want to give up, we have to somehow cherish life as much as we can.

Remember that things could always be worse. Because truthfully, all you really have is your life. Nothing or no one else is or should be more important.

End of the Road

*L*ife is not to be lived to amuse others. It's lived for you to enjoy. Why do so many people live their lives based on what others expect from them? I really don't know. I know so many people right now that are sitting in a cell, wishing they would have stayed home or simply would have not committed the act that got them locked up. Many people ask me what it is that made me change and I really don't have an answer for them. It's not like change happened overnight, but I truly feel that one of the things that played a really important role in the difference I have made in my life was other people's consequences. When I pictured myself in the shoes of those who stood in front of the judge being sentenced and then being led away in handcuffs that alone lets me know that no crime or illegal act is worth committing. My life is hard enough to live. I'm not trying to make it any harder by stressing in prison over some stupid choice I shouldn't have even thought about making.

Many times I look back and wonder why I was chosen to be one of the lucky ones to survive the streets. Sometimes I even wonder how I never got shot or ended up in prison after so many of the people I hung around with did. As bad as this may sound, I think that after seeing so many people get locked up or having to deal with so many people that I knew die, I have learned to appreciate my life a lot more than I ever have. Due to the fact that I had been hanging in the streets for so many years now, I know for sure that none of those people you see out there in the streets really mean when they say that they don't care if they are locked up or dead. They may act like it or even say it in words, but the moment those handcuffs are put on their wrists or the bullets go flying, it's a whole different story. I was never the craziest one to hang out on the streets. I never even made it to being one of the biggest drug dealers on the corner, either. One thing is for sure though, most that I did hang out on the streets with wish they could be where I am at today.

The rush of making money or committing crimes will eventually wear off once you have been locked up for a few months. Once you sit back and realize what you have done to ruin your life and your future, that's when reality hits you hard. I know many people till this day that act like they don't care about life or their freedom. But those same people have no problem with telling on others once they find themselves cornered. These days, I think I know more snitches than I do criminals and drug dealers. And that's adding the criminals and drug dealers together. If some of these people ever found out who the snitches were, they wouldn't even believe it. And in most cases, they really don't. They will continue to hang out together because they feel that they have really built a strong enough bond that they can trust each other to the very end. Let the judge offer one of them ten years or more and you'll definitely see a change of heart.

From the outside looking in, I now see the dangers I faced every time I stood out in the streets. I feel like I have no regrets because I never got to the point where I suffered from having to do time or having been shot. I can only imagine my life today if I would have ended up with a long criminal history. I struggle enough as it is now without having one. Another reason why I don't regret my past is because I have learned so much from it. Although I would probably be doing a lot better now, I also realize that I'm blessed not to be doing worse. You can pick one of the many crimes I committed that I never got caught for and you can probably add up to about at least twenty years in prison if not more. Out of all the crimes that I committed, most where committed against people I felt deserved it. In other words, at that point in time in my life, if I felt I was crossed the wrong way or you had something we were all struggling to get, chances were one of us would have tried to take it from you. The best thing was that I committed most of my crimes alone, and the few that I committed with others were always kept quiet. Back then people didn't tell on each other as much as they do today.

Although at times my life is not as fun as it was when I was living the street life, I can honestly admit that I love my life and the way I've turned out. It is a hell of a lot better than being locked up, being drug tested, having a curfew, being told what to do every day, bouncing from house to house because I can't afford to live on my own, or being homeless. These are some examples of the kinds of situations I see people going through today. These examples have always been my fears. It scares the hell out of me to ever have to deal with any of those issues. It's these physical regrets that people go through that make them mentally weak to bounce back from. Once they feel that even family has given up on them or that society would never accept them, the chances of changing their ways may no longer be an option. That's where you get the large number of inmates and drug addicts we have today.

Today, I have more people on my side that I know will be very disappointed if I ever went back to the streets. I also know that there are many others who would love to see me fail only to say that they always knew I was a loser just like them. But I don't have anything to prove to anyone except to myself. The freedom of being able to open up my own doors and go wherever the hell I want is good enough for me. It is much easier to sit around good people where we can talk and laugh and not have to worry about offending each other. It's better than standing around others not knowing if I can't trust them with a secret, never mind my life. I just can't imagine losing my freedom forever over an act that took just seconds to commit. It just doesn't add up.

People Pleaser

*W*hile many continue to claim that things happen for a reason, I feel the complete opposite is true. Things in my life have not happened for good reasons. Why? Because I figure the things that others wanted, I never really needed. And the things that others needed, I never really wanted. I never chose anything in my life just to be the center of attention like most have. It almost seemed to me as if people were always afraid of not accomplishing things such as having kids or being married before reaching a certain age. This leads me to these questions. What motivates you to be you? Is it the satisfaction you get from how others perceive you or the pleasure of who you make them think you are? For example, think of the reasons why people may like you or dislike you. Do they only like you because they are somehow benefiting from you or is it because they really do care for who you are? What about when it comes to disliking you? Do they dislike or hate you because they're not getting what they feel they should from you or is it because they haven't taken the time to really get to know the real you?

Here's where the answers to these questions may lay. Ask yourself these questions. Do you live only to please others or are you being true to yourself with everything you do? Are you pleasing people with what you think they want to hear or are you truthful and honest regardless of whether they may be offended or not? Bottom line is, regardless of the choices you make in life, the truth will always come out in the end. What makes that even scarier is that just when you think you know it all, there are always going to be new lessons to learn from or deal with. The one thing I had to learn from these situations was to limit the amount of people I had around me. You can't assume that everyone in front of you are all there for the same reasons. Everyone has an angle. It is your choice to pick and choose the people you feel you can trust but it's not in your control to avoid anything that occurs after that.

I have big issues with my short-term goals. One of the biggest mistakes that for some reason or another I continue making and keep getting the same results is feeling that I have to lower my standards to please people I care about and thinking that they are going to appreciate having someone like me. I get so caught up with assuming I'm going to change the person's way of thinking when they may just be fully satisfied and comfortable with who they are. The thoughts of being used have also crossed my thoughts as well. I'm not saying I'm better than most of the people I come across. What I am saying is that sometimes I truly feel like people take someone like me for granted. The mistake I make is that I sometimes miss the whole point. Because I'm more focused on them changing who they are instead of understanding what I'm dealing with. Lately though, I get the feeling that I may just be dealing with the wrong crowd. My lifestyle has changed over the past few years, but the types of people I keep running into have not. And the harder I try to change people to be or think like me, the more I realize that people are going to continue to do what they think works for them. *Just like I did in my past.*

No one will ever change unless they want to. That becomes even more obvious when they show you their true colors in the end. Some people don't want to be bothered with advice. Most will claim that they are tired of hearing it but still continue to beg for help when they're stuck in a bad situation. The only time they seem to agree with anything you ever tell them is when you finally take care of their problems. Next week, you'll be arguing about the same shit all over again. There are some people out there that know how to use their unfortunate situations as a tool to get the things they want or need. Some will cry on your shoulder, some will be extra friendly with you, and some may even use sex to confuse you with true love just to get what they want. And you can tell they are experts at doing these things because when you try to leave them they show no signs of even caring. They just pick up right where they left off with you and find someone else to fool.

I have fewer issues with my long-term goals. What seems to work for me is very simple. Regardless of how many choices I may have or a certain deadline for me to make a decision by, my main focus is on the possible outcomes or consequences I may have to deal with. I guess it's similar to how you should always think before you speak. The biggest mistake you can ever make is to never take the time to think where a decision may lead you. The problem is that when it comes to choices everyone seems to only think about the ones that will bring to them the quickest results. But not everything in life is about bene-fiting. It's also about the lessons you learn from the out-come of every choice and decisions you have made in order to never make the same mistakes again. These lessons will eventually make you wise enough to give advice to others you may have to deal with in your future. Whether it's a friend, a family member, and most importantly, when you become a parent.

If you only limit yourself to doing the things you have always done, you will never grow as a person. You will continue living the same stressful life and dealing with the same results and consequences. I don't consider myself a victim or even cry when things go wrong. You have to sometimes laugh at yourself and understand that you are the fool for thinking that you are in control of things you may never be able to change. That could be a problem in itself, but sticking around and continuing to stress your-self out by giving in would be worse. I have realized that some of the hardest things in life to let go of are the people you think you could change. Everyone views things dif-ferently. Not everyone's view of the world is the same. People may not be satisfied with their situations, and just choose to never change them. But like they say, you never know what you had until you lose it. But how does a loser know what they have lost when they never knew what it was like to gain?

Black-Hearted

For those who think that I don't have any feelings or think I only care about myself, they could be right. For the past few years, I have realized that the number of friends and even family members who have actually stood by my side in my time of need has shrunk to almost none. Now that I keep to myself and don't bother with getting involved in their issues, they assume that I think I'm better than them. It does seem as though I have become a little anti-social to most. But in reality, I have learned that everything in life has to go both ways. Like I have said before, it's not so much that I expect things in return; I just want my efforts to be noticed. Instead, it almost feels like my help is expected rather than appreciated. I will be honest about one thing: I didn't just become an asshole overnight. My own friends with a little help from some family members helped me become the best asshole that I could possibly be.

I think it's funny how when I react to people's ignorance or stupidity, I'm considered a loser in their eyes. Whenever I was in a position to help or give, I never thought twice about it. Anyone that has ever been close to me can't deny that. I have learned to respect people's privacy, as well as their personal business. I feel that once you cross the line of disrespecting those two things, there is really no way to make up for it. Here are some examples: If someone tells you not to call them, don't call. If someone tells you they don't want to see you, don't just show up at their home or at their job. If someone tells you things aren't working out, don't try to force them to change their mind. If you feel that someone is a loser or isn't worth your time, leave them alone and move the fuck on. Why would you want to try to make something out of nothing? I know that if someone tells me to leave them alone or they no longer feel a certain way about me, I have to respect that. Going crazy over it to the point where it becomes a legal issue is definitely taking it too far.

Life isn't fair. There are going to be times in life when people are going to make you feel worthless or cheated.

I've had a few shares of it myself. Not to say I have never made anyone feel the same way, but I want someone to explain one thing to me. If there is no way to change a person's mind once it is made up, why do people feel the need to even question it? Relationships between people aren't mandatory. There are no laws or contracts that have to be met before you decide to move on. No one literally steals your heart or owes you time back when you feel you have wasted it. Yes, it does hurt. We all know that. Forcing people to feel how you feel is only going to make you drift further apart. Shit, they might go from not liking you to hating you even more.

Honestly, I really don't care about that many people like I once used to. I understand that's a very harsh thing to say, but I really do mean it. People act like they don't give a fuck about me, so why should I bother with them? It's funny how people act like they don't know what happened between you and them when you decide to stop speaking to them. They always act like they did nothing wrong or say that I always seem to overreact. But I'm not the kind of person who goes around talking shit about people or saying disrespectful things to them in front of others. When people do that to me, the first thing I feel like doing is picking up the closest thing to me and breaking it on their face. But I know that would be overreacting just a little. So in order for me not to end up doing something crazy or ending up in a courtroom, I just simply part ways with them.

I put way too much effort into family and friendships. As a matter of fact, I do way more for the people around me then they would do for me all together. So when I feel like someone is crossing the line of disrespect, I do take it very personal. I didn't tolerate it from anyone while I was out in the streets so why should I start now? I guess people feel that just because I stopped living the street life that now they can speak about me or disrespect me how they want and I won't react. In most cases I won't because nothing is worth me going to prison just to prove a point. I may be a loser in many people's eyes, but one thing I'm not going to lose is my freedom over their ignorance. I would much rather walk away from a situation than lose my freedom. Back in the day I would have risked it all over respect.

At the end of the day: no matter how real I should have been to myself, I was always real to everyone I came across. You would have always known how much I liked you or even how much I didn't. I've never been the kind to hold back from expressing how I felt. And although many of my closest friends may have expected a lot more from me, I did my best. I gave to everyone what I felt they deserved. I treated you the same way you treated me. If you didn't like the way I responded or reacted then maybe you should have thought twice about putting me in that situation. Last, but definitely not least, if you didn't like me or the way I lived, too fucking bad. If you paid as much attention to your own life as you did to me, you wouldn't be standing next to someone you consider a loser. Because in the end, that just makes two of us.

Louder Than Words

*W*hen people are at their weakest state of mind, they tend to contradict their own words and thoughts. They second guess themselves wondering between how they will benefit if things go their way versus how much they will regret if things don't prior to making up their minds. The most challenging situations are the ones we really want to see work in our favor but become harder to achieve. Rather than being patient, people tend to focus more on the outcome instead of the risk.

Most of the time when people claim that they don't care about a person or a situation they are currently experiencing difficulties with is usually when they care the most. In the heat of the moment the words that are being expressed are usually out of anger due to not having things go their way. If a person really didn't care, then it would have been a lot easier to move on. They wouldn't be wasting all their time and energy going back and forth about their issues unless they wanted the outcome to be different. But if you go back to a situation and pick up where you left from, why are you expecting a different outcome? Wouldn't that just be continuing the situation?

I don't know why people act so surprised when they see a person ask for advice, agree with everything they are told, even fully understand it all, and then turn around and do the complete opposite. I call it "advice versa." Chances are they already knew deep inside what their decision was going to be. I have been there many times before. I second-guess my decisions all the time. Like they say, desperate times call for desperate measures. Truly speaking though, it should never matter what others tell you. The only reason others may give you alternatives is because they don't want to see you getting hurt. But the decision will always be yours. If you choose not to listen, you'll be the one suffering from the consequences all on your own.

Most of the time when a person asks for advice is because they are caught in between confusing choices. Not because they don't know what to do. In my opinion there are two reasons why. They either want a little security by checking to see how many people will agree or to know how they would look in advance in the eyes of others before making their decision. Anytime a person has a hard decision to make they tend to lean more toward how much they will lose if they chose to part ways. Instead, what they should do is focus more on where their decisions will lead them. Unfortunately, this is the part of life where you will never know regardless of the choice you make. Eventually, you will begin to second-guess yourself by wondering what the outcome would have been if you had made a different choice.

Most people really can't handle the truth. They always think they can change the outcome of certain things that they should just accept for what they are. The only choice they truly have is to whether they want to deal with it or not. Nothing makes you go through this more than a love-hate relationship. Hate tends to have more drama and carries more energy and strength. That's why we react the way that we do when things don't go as planned. Love is too easy. It's too peaceful. Love does outweigh hate many times though and that's why it makes people do stupid things over it. Expressing how you really feel deep inside shouldn't make you look or feel stupid, but reacting in a foolish way will. If things are meant to be, they will be... If they are not, time will tell. Why force a situation just to be satisfied physically but have to struggle with it mentally?

The first time that a person shows you their true colors is when you have to begin to accept that person for what they are and not who they claim to be. Never consider their actions or reactions to being a mistake or accident. That alone will pretty much tell you the kind of person you will be dealing with until they decide if they want to change or not. Many people hold back and wait to show their truest feelings until they are being rejected somehow. You have to accept the fact that you are the creator of your own problems when you allow your feelings to take over or get in the way. Don't just consider yourself the victim when someone doesn't want to deal with the way you are responding. Imagine the situation from the other side and see how you would react if they were treating you how you are treating them.

One of the best ways to judge how much you truly care is by drawing a line between the positives and the negatives. The positives in a person or a situation are already there. That's why you are so attracted to them. But if you can take one negative at a time and turn it into a positive rather than to just hate the negatives overall and do anything except judge a person by them, how can you ever say that you cared? Trying to force people or things to change is the main reason why it may not work out in your favor in the end. You also have to take the time to understand why people and things are the way that they are. Not to say that it must be a good reason or excuse. In fact, it may also be what drives a person to cheat or leave you.

Ground Zero

*A*fter all these years and everything that I've been through, I have to say that it was all worth it. Although I live with many regrets, I have accepted not only who I am today but also where I stand. I have learned many valuable lessons and I know that many more will come. That's life. It's not only what you make of it but also how you choose to continue living it. It was unfortunate that many good people had to suffer while I was transitioning and changing my way of life. They couldn't understand that I was stuck between two lives when I responded in the ways that I did instead of the ways they thought I should have. I was treating the good people in my life the same way I was treating those in the streets. I had a very hard time trying to change not only who I was but also the way I dealt with my issues.

It was very hard for me to accept the fact that I had to change if I wanted things to be different. It was even harder for me to accept trust and those who claimed to be honest because where I came from those two things were what ended up getting many people killed. When those that you trusted as friends have lied, cheated, and stole from you, how easy could it have been to accept friendship from anyone? How do you trust a person that claimed they loved you but also did the same? I felt I had no other options and was tired of playing the victim. In fear of having these things continue hurting me, I set aside my feelings and just lived my life how I wanted to. It was a never-ending circle of situations that kept coming around because I didn't want to learn or accept the lessons I should have. It was hard for me to accept the fact that not everyone was out to hurt me.

Although I have become desensitized to the many issues others dread going through, it was those lessons that have made me who I am today. I've seen and been through so much that people close to me find it hard to believe that I deal with things different from others who show their feelings publicly. It's sad that I have to admit that at one point in my life many dangerous situations became more entertaining for us than they were life-threatening. But I knew that there were only so many chances that I could continue taking before the consequences caught up to me. If the things that I was experiencing on the daily basis didn't make me change, the advice from people did even less.

Sometimes I wonder how the hell I made it to this point in life. I wonder even more how I made it back home each day and night. It's very confusing to me because I never prepared for anything that I am actually going through now. I never planned anything. Things seem to have just fallen in place for me, as if everything I did in my past was the training to get me to where I am at today. I look back and think of the days when those bullets missed me. How those cops never caught me when I ran. Although I did love the rush of it all, I always did fear getting caught. Lucky for me, they were all a bad shot. Everyone around me swallowed crack to avoid being arrested. Me, I just dodged bullets and bullshit all day. I always felt like as long as I lived in fear of getting caught or shot every day that it would keep me on my toes. I never got too comfortable like those who thought life in the street was going to last forever. I can still remember walking by cops with enough drugs on me to put me away for years. Yet I can still look back and call it the "Good Ol' days."

My biggest fear of changing my ways was always thinking that people were going to view it as a weakness. For some reason, I was always offended and I cared about what people said about me. But one day, I decided that I was not just going to continue reacting to the things people were saying; I was going to pay closer attention to it instead. Because in most cases, what people say about you does have a bit—if not a lot—of truth to it. Especially if a lot of people are saying it. So instead of getting mad or finding a way to explain myself, I took the rumors about me less personally and used them to learn about what I may have been doing wrong. There is nothing wrong with having to hear what people say about you. In some cases they could actually be describing you in many ways that others who are afraid to tell you think about you as well. Responding to rumors only made me look guilty. But the only thing I was really guilty of was giving people a reason to judge me for my own actions. So I had to also accept that I was partly to blame for giving people those options.

Anything that people ever had to say about me before today has a great chance of it all being true. I am man enough to admit that. But I'm no politician so airing my dirty laundry won't affect or offend me. I'm guilty of a lot of things many people are still doing today. There are many who were just like me and many more that will continue that cycle. There were hundreds of things that I did wrong. So to judge me for a few of them is actually a compliment. Where I came from you had to get dirty to get what you wanted. Everybody had what you wanted and you wanted what everyone had. That's the game in a nutshell. Anyone I knew or came across who spoke about me in any negative way was a hypocrite.

I am now back to square one a "New Beginning". The best part is that I'm still here. I have sifted through everything I've have been through and have taken and accepted the good with the bad. What else can I do? Living in regret every day and wishing I could change everything overnight is not only impossible but also a waste of time. The only thing I am in control of is not repeating what I have been through. You are more than welcome to critique the things that I have written. You are entitled to your own opinions or what you may already consider facts. But in order to judge anyone you also have to accept the fact that you can always be judged as well. I learned a lot from being a loser. I've made many choices in my life that may have not been the smartest. But how smart are you to make choices that will not have you regretting your decisions? Learn to live happily, give and accept love, and remember to laugh even when the joke is on you. Remember that times could always be worse.

In Closing: Loser

*N*ow that you have read every poor excuse and all of my reasons for the way that I have dealt with my issues, you now know more about what being a loser really means. I used to get offended every time someone tried to interfere with what I always thought was my better judgment. It wasn't so much that I really knew it all; I just became used to a personality that only had me losing everything and everyone that was very valuable to me. It took me staring into the mirror one day and realizing that I was at fault for most—if not all—of the negative outcomes in my life. I blamed everything on everyone else and never stopped to think that I dealt with matters in ways that others couldn't handle. I have learned that lessons are not about winning or losing; it's about understanding.

It is very unfortunate that I have become so good at knowing "how not to be" but can't make it up to those I have lost. They truly meant so much. I always thought that

I was put on this earth to just suffer, but I have realized that it was I who chose that path. Now I am lost without a roadmap. I have been very contrary in my life. I always knew what was better for me. I always wanted things my way—and that was my downfall. I never thought that what others expected from me mattered. I thought that as long as I could keep them near, I was doing what was beneficial to me. That is Loser mentality at its best. It's sad but so true that you never really know what you had until you are on the receiving end of all the wrongs you made others suffer.

Where do I go from here? Where do I begin? Who is going to give me another opportunity to prove myself to them? It's sad that I have to admit this, but the real question is, why should they? I don't blame anyone but myself for the way people have turned their backs on me. I can't blame anyone for never wanting to give me the opportunity to show them that I have changed. If you have never experienced loneliness in your life, I would never wish it upon you. It is not a safe place to be—mentally or physically. It's like living in two different worlds or having split personalities. Unfortunately, the wrong side of my double life won. I ignored the whispering voices in my head that kept telling me to do right.

From this moment in my life all the way up until the very last breath I take, I will try to prove to myself that I can do it the right way. If no one is willing to give me the opportunity to show to them that I am ready, then I will just have to accept that, and keep going. I'm not ready to give up just yet. There is always hope, as long as I can still hold on. I may not have the strength at this moment in my life, but I have faith. I hope that after all these years; everything that I have done wasn't a waste. I hope that everything was for a real good reason and not just for me to suffer from and regret. I will keep looking ahead and hoping that something good comes from all of my dealings and I will always cherish the good moments I've had.

To all the people that tried to show me the meaning of *Love*...I am sorry. I was too ignorant to accept it the way that I should have. I thought that you loving me was good enough. I felt that if I could continue to give you reasons to love me that you would stand by my side forever. I am now very aware that's not the way it should have been. If you ever find yourself in a situation where your thoughts and your heart are confusing you, don't fear it.

It's called *Love*.

CPSIA information can be obtained
at www.ICGtesting.com
Printed in the USA
BVOW06*0934020118
504197BV00012B/573/P